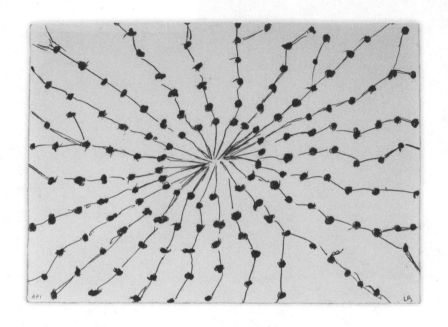

PHILIPPE DELERM

Second Star

and Other Reasons for Lingering

TRANSLATED FROM THE FRENCH BY
Jody Gladding

archipelago books

Library of Congress Cataloging-in-Publication Data available upon request.
ISBN 9781953861542

Archipelago Books
232 3rd Street #A111
Brooklyn, NY 11215
www.archipelagobooks.org

Distributed by Penguin Random House
www.penguinrandomhouse.com

Cover art: Pierre Bonnard
Book design by Gopa & Ted2, Inc.

This work was made possible by the New York State Council on the Arts with the
support of the Office of the Governor and the New York State Legislature.

This publication was made possible with support from Lannan Foundation,
the Carl Lesnor Family Foundation, the National Endowment
for the Arts, and Centre National du Livre.

Printed in Canada

Table of Contents

Translator's Note

THESE PIECES ARE drawn from *The Troubled Waters of the Mojito* and *The Ecstasy of the Selfie*, the most recent collections of Philippe Delerm's "literary snapshots," a genre he invented over two decades ago and still uniquely represents. One great joy in translating them was the empirical research they involved. For the rare piece that didn't prompt immediate recognition, I found myself, for instance, rolling up my sleeves, studying a mojito, trying a raw turnip—a caveat here, unless it's a mild salad variety, a thin slice is probably plenty! Turnip notwithstanding, I urge readers to wash windows, peel clementines, or run a hand over a book, especially *this* book, as much as you like. My endless thanks to Philippe Delerm for noticing. And to French and American publishers, Seuil and Archipelago, for making this English translation possible.

SECOND STAR

Le vrai bonheur serait de se souvenir du present.

—JULES RENARD

The Lie of the Watermelon

I T'S TOO BEAUTIFUL. Strange. Do you drink it? Eat it? It's like desire gone wrong. The reddish-pink of the bruised flesh, evanescent and bursting with water, fades to a sickly pallor along the edge of the tough, deep green, outer rind. At the center, it is so dark, embedded with worrisome seeds, ebony black. Seeds or poisoned spear tips?

How is it possible to be that heavy with so much shameless, lavish nothingness? Always on display at summer markets, the watermelon poses as ultimate recourse for a thirst that's never quenched. What's the point of buying it? You already sense that it'll dissolve on the tongue, crimson snow melting much too fast. The mango and guava taste like mango and guava. The watermelon doesn't taste like anything, and that's why you desire it, in vain. It is the perfection of its lie, and the produce vendors know that. They display it by itself, acknowledging the role it plays. It attracts all the attention, brazenly combines coolness and sweat, imparts a bit of its elusive perfection to the modest fruits around it.

Shamelessly it sells itself. You don't buy it, for fear of ridicule. You know in advance that you could not truly possess it. Its taste is transparent. It's only a mirage of heat and summer.

The Embarrassment of Vaping

SMOKING IS BAD. Terrible for you, as well as for others. That idea was established with much effort and much difficulty. More than dissuasive slogans, more than apoplectic photos of ravaged mucous membrane, the anonymity of cigarette packs may have dealt the final blow. Or almost. But it's clearly with regard to the gestural that smoking has suffered its greatest losses. With vaping, public acknowledgment of the addiction has taken on a more furtive, more shameful appearance. One doesn't even dare say that an e-cigarette is smoked. It's imbibed, off to the side, head bent, eyes averted. It's like the makeshift subterfuge of bygone days, adolescents in school corridors concealing under their jackets, between drags, their lit cigarettes, a free hand fanning the sluggish curls of smoke.

Although vaping isn't hidden. Whereas lighting up calls for a form of withdrawal, almost a retreat. A priori, each object requires its own, purely physical, expression. But we can't help adding a social dimension, unconsciously slipping in a little ethics. By its very nature, the electronic cigarette is an ersatz cigarette. With it, dependency can never be triumphant. The real cigarette looms, in diaphanous and cumbersome suspense, over its replacement. It was incarnated—is incarnated still—in various mythologies, in postures ranging from the most hardened masculinity to the most mysterious femininity. It was—and still is—both Humphrey Bogart and Lauren Bacall. It's forever that mushroom cloud of intelligence hovering over the broadcasts of Bernard Pivot and Michel Polac. It's Gainsbourg devolving into his caricature Gainsbarre, a Gitanes smoker jeering at death. His style and eloquence have the charm of a savored suicide.

There's none of that with vaping. At first it was thought to be harmless, quite an insult to a self-destructive ritual. Doubts were raised, which have yet to spawn a new mythology. That's because of the gesture. So sad in its asceticism, its privacy, surly

Epicurean reduced to Jansenist. Someday maybe there'll be a Gainsbourg for vaping. Although it's hard to imagine. In the meantime, we have to go on living, or else smoking. Because smoking kills. But then living does too.

His Lips Barely Move

Y**OU'RE WITH HIM** on the bus. Well, with him? Sitting just across from you, he's here, elsewhere, everywhere. He is seven years old. The first year of elementary school. And this year, he really knows how to read. A few minutes ago, hardly out of the bookstore, he seized Yvan Pommaux's little book with the lavender blue cover and immediately set off, vaguely aware of the reality around him—avoiding pedestrians a bit like a slalom skier makes his way between gates. Often people passing him smiled. And you feel rather proud to have an avid reader for a grandson.

Now, in the jolting traffic, you watch him in his bubble, so far away, so close. What's fascinating is the imperceptible movement of his lips. He doesn't wrinkle his forehead or knit his brow. But he's not yet gliding effortlessly through the course. He has to do this deciphering, not yet completely fluid, exalted by his drive, his passion, his moving desire to possess the world he wants to escape into.

You're sure that if you were reading that story to him, he'd smile often. But he isn't smiling. He looks intent, serious. He's creating his own lands of adventure, the quiet secret of his distance. His lips move. With small sips he's drinking in the difficult magic of the breakaway.

It's still work, and it's already freedom. There's a code. You don't disturb him with questions like, "Do you like it? Is it good?" You know that sleepwalkers must not be taken by surprise. Nor do you want to bring him back to reality, the presence of a grandfather with his grandson on a crowded bus in the late afternoon. You get to fly by watching him fly. He has never looked so beautiful to you. His lips barely move.

Holding a Glass of Wine

YOU HAVE A glass of wine in your hand, three fingers holding the bowl, thumb toward you, index and middle finger facing out, ring and little finger not needed for this scene. Because it is a performance, straight off, a posture—even and especially if you pretend to be looking elsewhere, to be deep in conversation. It's all delectable.

Such a tall glass could seem precarious, but its roundness sits squarely in a firm hand that hides and seems to protect the red or white wine—it's almost always red. This is an evening gesture, best when there are two of you, when words can be well spaced, leaving room for wide swaths of silence. Maybe you'll have dinner, or not really. Maybe you've already eaten, not very much, and that was a long time ago, you only drank water.

It's better when it's dark outside. You wander from room to room, lamps low, scattered books. You put on soft music: *Pavane pour une infante défunte*, the perfect score for an evening that's meant to last, that lasts.

Sometimes, when you're on the elevated railway, you pass very close to apartments, and you see a woman exit a room, glass in hand, as though to celebrate her time and place. You envy her calm, detached profile, her absence, framed by the open curtains. She has that way of leaving without going anywhere. Holding a glass of wine, contained within you are these old images you've glimpsed, that self-possession you've imagined, all those distant pleasures silhouetted against the traffic.

You aren't having a drink. You hold a glass in your hand. You haven't tasted the wine, or just barely, you don't remember anymore, it doesn't really matter. What matters is the holding, the holding back, the deferring, the not starting in, that's the whole game. Where does this power come from? Every waking moment, in the very depths of each sleepless night, you've felt swallowed by time. And here you are in command, simply because the wine is there for the taking, and you haven't downed it, you won't let yourself taste or even smell it. It's good to invent this distance from the goblet to the lips. But pleasure isn't the point; the wine won't improve with all the waiting. What's really good is being yourself, your hand so nicely rounded, how you become this vaguely flattering, elegant gesture that only seems unconscious, this eternal thirst that's never quenched.

Dancing Without Knowing How to Dance

A<small>T SUMMER FESTIVALS</small> during vacations in the country, you were among those who avoided dancing, not budging from your seat at the café table. You watched the pasodoble and rock-and-roll dancers, admiring their ease and ability. You loved them so much because you didn't know how to dance. Later, you were among those who didn't go to nightclubs. And now here you are. Life has passed. You find yourself at a wedding. In general they bore you, these efforts at conversation with the bride's cousins you'll never see again. So when the music begins, you opt instead to dance.

Dance: that's a big word. You move like a bear. But who cares. You're too old to be self-conscious. And you're in luck, they're starting off with a twist. You can make the most of your inadequacies, bending your knees, moving your arms in a way that doesn't fool anyone but seems to be mocking a whole era—yours. The problem is that right beside you some much younger dancers have perfectly mastered the twist. Oh well, this isn't a competition.

A waltz! There again, you can turn in circles wearing an ineffable smile. Alain Delon in *The Leopard*. Without showing it, you begin to feel strangely good. You become the characters you're pretending to imitate. Gradually you forget that anyone's watching. This is no longer parody, the risk of looking ridiculous seems to fade. You're making peace with your body. You see the perfect movements of those with real technique but, oddly, you don't envy them. They've always known how to dance, no doubt, and know nothing of the melancholy of not knowing. It's great to feel inferiority become superiority. Not knowing how to dance, you regard the practice as sacred, you grant it all its power. Apparently all those lost years are now culminating in your present happiness. And finally you're getting revenge for your shackled youth.

Memory at Your Fingertip

YOUR INDEX FINGER wanders over the tablet or smartphone screen. Images file by. Sometimes your finger stops, and deep within your eyes a smile forms. A bit of your recent past surfaces. Strange, this way of bringing forth and obliterating. The process would seem to require extreme care. At the surface, an incantation. A strange caress, with the tip of a single finger. You aren't exhuming or consulting. You're taming.

It really seems as though the smartphone or tablet has changed the nature of memory. There's nothing miraculous here; it was ordained, desired. Memories seem to obey. But it's not at all like a photo that you hold, adjust, glue at the four corners. Life is there, but on the other side of the screen. The finger that gives rise to it, that summons it and makes it disappear, only pretends to be in command. It touches without touching, it venerates, it grazes. It would like to weigh even less, to dissipate, to become just a breath.

And so it's the past that seems called into question. Did you really live or did you only brush past without connecting? There's some resignation in this infinitesimal ceremony, this silence. With the tip of your finger, you can only draw near. Or not even that. A kind of uncertainty remains in this so distant proximity. You can make all those you believe you've held, everything you believe you've done, glide across a mirror. With the tip of this single finger that wishes to scare away nothing. All this nothing comes at a cost.

You experience a kind of rarefaction, a kind of lassitude as well, from too much evanescence. It's so perfect, so detached. Children, loved ones, cherished landscapes succeed one another horizontally, leaving a trail across the rink as they skim past and are drowned. By the tip of the tip of the finger, under the surface of ice.

Shower

TUCKING YOUR HEAD, you hunched your shoulders. When the rain picked up, insolent, perverse—a whole patch of blue sky to the west, streets still sunlit—you frowned a bit theatrically. You stamped impatiently at the red light. You were already soaked. Over there, that little roof jutting out from the pharmacy. Then you made a run for it, felt the March chill penetrate your body. Just before the shelter, you slowed your pace. A smile crossed your lips, as though in self-mockery, such a pitiful sight for those already under cover.

And it's just those few seconds. You compose yourself. You take deep breaths, as if you'd just been saved from drowning or suffocation. The others squeeze in to make room for the new castaway. You thank them with a nod that acknowledges yes, we're all reduced to the same fate.

It's good, this imposed break. There's something rejuvenating in your exaggerated breathing, the coolness of the water drumming, there, so close. An icy drop escapes the roof and runs down your neck.

You don't talk to each other. A little discomfort just has time to set in before someone dispels it, saying, "I think it's beginning to let up." To avoid embarrassment, he'll decide to leave much too soon. Because it will keep raining as the sky clears, the idea of a rainbow preceding the rainbow. There's no hurry anymore. Now who was it who wrote that little prose poem with the final words you love? "And I'll go bring in the forgotten croquet set that's getting drenched."

What Authority!

IT'S BEEN FIFTEEN minutes since you sat down. All the surrounding tables are full. The music of conversation has taken on that calm amplitude that settles in when meals are served, when one of the diners exclaims parenthetically at the freshness of the vegetables. At first you're not worried, you're not in a big hurry. But even so, insidiously, the waiter's refusal to look your way begins to weigh on you. You try to catch his eye a few times without being obvious, without interrupting the anecdote you're telling. It's quite an art, this selective feverishness of the wait staff, attentive to the smallest details regarding the tables already "in hand" but struck blind when it comes to new customers, yet to be greeted, yet to be welcomed.

Not getting served is one thing. Seeing that others can see you're not getting served is something else again. In the game of sidelong glances, it's that minute pressure that will make you decide to try a gesture. Putting up with this too long might prompt commiseration, could threaten your standing. So you raise your hand, trying to be both commanding and discreet— and that's not easy. Too timid, and your signal will be drowned in the commotion of the room, inspiring conciliatory pity from the nearest table without fazing the perversely cool waiter. Too energetic, and your waving arm will be vulgar, ridiculous if it produces no effect, and unpleasant for your table companion who's talking and will think you've stopped listening. And then too, you don't want to create a forced relationship. Mutual regard between you and the waiter remains the hope, or it will have to be mutually feigned.

Your hand nears your lips with a kind of suspension, hesitation, discouraged weariness. At that moment, of course, the waiter discovers you. He blinks his eyes in your direction as if, until then, you've been hidden in a cloud of mist. To temper the audacity of your appeal, you'll search your voice's register for the smoothest, most civilized tone to ask: "Could we get a menu please?"

Second Star

ALMOST TEN O'CLOCK. The late July night takes its time set-
tling in, imparts a bit of mauve to the sky and the brown
sand. They're the last ones on the beach. Squeezed together
in a square like a small, entrenched camp, they've endlessly
delayed the moment for the picnic. They don't own a vacation
home and they aren't renting one, not even an apartment, that's
immediately obvious. Later, they'll have to pack into a car and
return inland. No, two cars, there must be at least a dozen of
them. The children played for a long time, letting out shrieks
of horror when, with a few waves, the tide destroyed the last of
the buttresses they'd built up by the shovelful. Let them make
the most of it, there's no hurry, they're good here.

In the distance, the terrace lights come on at the Grand Hotel.

Can't be too bad there, the ceremonial platters of seafood, the bottle of Sancerre beaded with icy sweat. But fine, let them battle with their crab legs. The cold chicken from the cooler is delicious, even better than at noon—a little wind was blowing sand then, the sun was beating down.

They ran, they swam, they got out rackets, balls, magazines. The men took naps, their faces in the shade of the beach umbrella. The old woman especially kept an eye on the others, a half-smile of camaraderie on her lips, offering a cheek for wet, hurried, distracted kisses. Now it's getting cooler. They huddle together, back to back. There are still apricots to eat. There are long silences. Yes, it was a lovely Sunday. Waiting for the last of the traffic to clear up at the Nantes bridge. Waiting, putting off tomorrow. Waiting for the dissipating joys to make way for the idea of happiness, which makes you shiver. It's just the night falling, pull on a sweater. Being so very much together, when others seem so very far away, and when you're all in a square protecting each other.

—Are you asleep, Leila?

—No, I'm waiting for the second star.

A Hip Move and Memory

O NE OF THE first gestures of the day, before starting coffee or turning on the radio. Almost a reflex. You opened the shutters and, in the same movement, drew back your right hip. You did this every time. The cat came in from his nightly roaming; he'd seen the light or had some secret sense that the house was coming back to life. It was still dark. The first few times, you were a little apprehensive, afraid of mutual clumsiness, of not giving the cat enough space, of being scratched. But no. Right from the start, the movement was perfect, the slightest brush along your thigh, an almost feigned hurry once it had become your ritual.

You greeted him with the kind of remark one feels obliged to utter in such cases, a routine joke about his supposed escapades.

The silence in response meant: if you're enjoying this little chat, fine, I know you're about to give me my milk. The roles were peacefully assigned in furry serenity, the day could begin.

Then, years had passed, the cat was dead. Suddenly one morning you said to yourself: "Still this little twist when I open the shutters, it's nuts. He's been dead at least two weeks!" With sadness was mixed a certain pride: "I've kept him here in my body. I haven't forgotten."

Of course, that's how the forgetting began. At first, no longer unthinkingly opening the shutters, but watching yourself do it, feeling the desire to shift your hip, immediately stopping yourself. The gesture is almost there, cultivating it would be obscene. And this cruel idea follows: none of this is under your control. You forgot the cat the moment you thought you'd always remember him.

The Sounds of Venice

OBVIOUSLY NOT on the Grand Canal, where the vaporetti, taxis, and barges loaded with merchandise perform their concert for water and engine. But everywhere else. Wafting through the calli, the sotoportegi, the campi.

A city where you can distinguish each sound is a city of silence. The music of voices, that drawling, lilting accent. Sometimes a familiarity that's a bit exaggerated because there's only time for a greeting: "Ciao Roberto! Ciao Francesca!"—but the insistence on the second syllable of the name gives a foreigner the feeling of clannish conviviality on a scale too vast to fathom. Most often, Venetians do have time to stop and chat with each other. A great many little old men and women with their caregivers. At Campo San Giacomo da l'Orio, they find themselves a spot on the flaking red benches, and they savor the melodic tangibility of their crisscrossing conversations. It's palpable. There's none of the henhouse bustle that you experience in France, even more so in the United States. In Venice, people listen with gusto to themselves and to one another. Even when voices are raised, the language remains sunny and supple.

On the paved square, you hear the echoes of balls bouncing, the cries of children splashing in fountains, scooters rolling by. Sounds that drift up toward the sky and say that everyone, old and young, has a place here.

If you listen carefully, you can make out the babble of a radio behind shutters drawn closed at the hottest hour of the day, and even the sound of a push broom sweeping dry leaves. So when evening comes in San Marco, you have no desire to seek out the bands with their syrupy accordions, pianos, violins. Let them float in the distance like mist, their easy charm dissolving in the night. You know that soon, very early tomorrow morning, you'll hear the voices of real life, when Venetians cross paths on their way to the vaporetto or the traghetto. "Ciao Roberto! Ciao Francesca!"

The Zone of Sorrow

YOU'LL SEEK OUT the temple. You'll glide the back of your finger across the cheek, very softly. Sitting face to face at a café table. There must be something separating you, enough distance for the movement of your arm to be slow, steady, ceremonial. You must know each other well, of course. A silence must have set in a few moments earlier, so that the surrounding conversations, their cheerfulness, have become almost insulting. You're inside your companion's sadness, it can't really be shared with words.

Will you meet with evasion, refusal, a turning away? You're sure that you won't, that you can risk it. There's a precise geography to respect. From temple to cheek, with the finger coming to rest well before the corner of the mouth. Yes, that's where this takes place. A gesture of sharing that means to bring comfort and harbors no illusions. The back of the finger traces a kind of soft scar, that acknowledges the sorrow and pain of living. This is the inside of a wound. You don't presume to try and dress it, you accompany it. I can feel, I think, what you're feeling, and I'm far enough away to want to be close. I pass the back of my index finger over this nearly abstract zone, where I'll touch neither your mouth nor your hair. I smile, just barely, with a such a sorry look, and you shake your head imperceptibly: yes, it's really hard, nothing will change that, but touch my cheek anyway—it's all you can do, thanks for knowing that. This is no longer silence; it's so much better than talking.

Still Life

THERE'S FRUIT: apples, grapes. Vegetables: asparagus, leeks,
for the tapering confusion of whites, off-whites, soft and
deep greens, blues heightened by the secret of mauve. There
are often fish, for the endless shimmering of icy grays shift-
ing almost to black. Cool tones over warm browns of kitchen
tables. There are fabrics, sometimes just the smooth folds of
dish towels strewn about in staged disarray. There are pewter
dishes, porcelain dishes, faceted crystal goblets in which red
wine glows with a burst of sunlight. There's the sensation of
touch, the astonishing power to recreate for the eye that imperceptible irritation peach skin produces.

There's that great silence, that immobility. Not a hand, not a
gesture, not the shadow of a silhouette. Things for the things

themselves, then? No. Things to be painted and, immediately after, to be eaten. As though painting was not the desire to immortalize, but rather to live and to devour life. We are in a seventeenth- or eighteenth-century kitchen—or maybe one closer to us, where Cézanne brazenly ignites his autumn apples.

In still lifes there are rituals we can recognize, of course, all those bourgeois preparations. The present must soon be consumed. We burn ourselves on a candlestick's suspended flame while the candle cracks and drips.

A Clementine, One-Handed

A CLEMENTINE IS the right size. It curls up in your hand and finds its exact place there. You test it with your thumb; it feels neither hard nor soft. Its slightly grainy skin is pleasant, no sophisticated smoothness, not rough. You can take it anywhere. It slides easily into the bottom of your bag, doesn't leave a stain, doesn't weigh a thing. And you can extract it at any moment, preferably a quiet one. Eating a clementine is a ritual that everyone around you agrees to—a little pause you're granted, restriction-free, prompting no disgust when traveling by car or by train.

The ultimate pleasure is beginning to peel it with one hand, doing this without looking, while continuing to read a book or check your phone. When the skin's too thin, it resists a little, but normally it has an obliging suppleness. It's worth noting the central filament: carefully preserved when the clementine's eaten at home, so it can be the wick of the small lantern you'll make from the intact peel, it must be torn out and sacrificed when you're on the go.

A seemingly impossible feat, and nonetheless you always manage it. You hold the entire peel and the fruit in your palm. A light, fresh fragrance begins to be released. You know that it doesn't bother others, it brings them memories of school before evening studies, or winter holidays. That's the moment to relinquish your indifference and devote both hands to separating the segments. Here again, the clementine doesn't play the flirt. Its accommodating nature recalls *Paul and Virginia*, that novel's world in which melons were ribbed so that humans could cut them into satisfying slices. But in the mouth, this prepackaged, well-behaved fruit nevertheless explodes; it quenches your thirst, appeases your hunger, and leaves suspended throughout whole train cars this troubling question: is it the clementine that smells like Christmas, or Christmas that smells like the clementine?

Wet Paint!

IT'S A CLUMSY sign, handwritten on a piece of cardboard in wavery block letters. On a bench, on a door, window, or gate. Be careful not to get paint on you. But also be careful not to spoil my paint job.

Either way, take notice. Otherwise you might well sit down there, or pass by without seeing it. It hasn't been destroyed, it hasn't been replaced. It's been repainted. Repainting: it's done with a light heart, whistling. Without pretending to change the universe, to make something new from something old. Although . . . Under its two coats of cart blue paint, the wood is much better than new. It still has the same knots, the same ridges. In repainting it, you're doing more than looking at it. Thanks to the tip of the paintbrush, you bond with its deep structure. First you feel the difficulty of penetrating it, then the surprise of seeing reality obey without submitting to you.

It's the month of March or April, when the sun has almost become warm. A neighbor stops in passing, "So, you're taking advantage of the good weather!" Another whom you hardly know, "That's a lot of work!" And a third, admiring the gate, "You're giving it a face-lift!"

You feel invested, like a guardian. You like things just as you've found them, even the most ornate, the least useful, the least functional. You're after those lives before yours, you want to make them your own, to embrace the decor and make it pleasing. Gently to astonish. To feel this little approval from the world and to give fair warning. Take notice, there's not much to see, but it's life I've changed. Wet paint!

Agreeing Without Knowing to What

THE WORDS JUST spoken don't matter. What counts is that you weren't asked for a specific response, no promise to meet or follow orders, not even for the future. No, those words required only perfunctory assent, or even just some proof that you were really listening. Often the one talking is satisfied with that. You agreed in the most neutral way possible, without enthusiasm, without trepidation, without smiling.

You began by nodding your head. Nothing unusual about that, but why are you still doing it? And now you're feeling that, deep within, something has changed. Your nod that was supposed to be a gesture of encouragement soon dissipates into a meditative—no, melancholic—fog. This slight bobbing is accompanied by a vacant, faraway look. As though resigned.

You agree. To what has just been said, yes, but even more: to what you are, to what's in store for us, and to an inner fatigue that escapes despite itself. Nothing serious, but even so, a way of saying that everything's laid out, irrevocable, insipid. Too acceptable, and much too accepted. Often you close the sequence by leaning your head to one side for a fraction of a second and raising your eyebrows in an almost palpable evocation of doubt or uncertainty, but even more, of consent to that doubt and uncertainty. And it's not so bad, all things considered, to be sure of nothing, to be alive and to agree without really knowing to what.

Thank you Isabelle Carré.

Palming It

W HAT A MANLY gesture! Preferably performed during a slightly delicate maneuver when classic concentration with hands firmly grasping the wheel would seem to be required. With a cool expression and often a wad of chewing gum, a kind of additional metaphor for coolness on display, the palm driver executes his great feat. He doesn't need his fingers. His mastery over the vehicle is in the skin, in the heel of the hand. A grand revolution of the steering wheel in one direction, then in the other. It's James Bond parallel parking.

There's the idea of lightness in this plan—I press gently on the surface of things and they obey me. Nevertheless, strangely, this desire for a light touch harbors an arrogant and slightly brutal violence. That's because of the displayed open palm: the sensuality of the tough guy who considers other men cowards and thinks that women find their driver's licenses in detergent boxes. Obviously it's possible to drive without using one's fingers. But that gesture, which wants so badly to say that I'm stronger, more relaxed, cleverer, faster than you, instantly inspires disdain rather than the admiration this show-off desires. He knows very well that he's being seen. Seen badly.

A Summer Evening

THE END of June. We're going to have dinner in the garden. We set out candles almost everywhere, on the window sills, in the branches of the old quince and apple trees. At the stroke of ten we pull on sweaters, but it's not cold, and everyone wants to stay longer. We've all had a bit too much to drink, but our friends live five hundred meters away, they walked over. Friends for almost our whole lives, completely at ease. We savor the few moments of silence, after the cheese and last glass of Saint-Joseph—I like this wine a lot, it has a kind of soft warmth.

In a few minutes, bats have chased off the June bugs with their inoffensive buzz. The exasperating scent of honeysuckle. You're staying here in July? Yes, at least until the twenty-third.

So, yes, we can add to the peace of this evening the certainty that there will be others like it, as easy, as light.

Certainty? The moment the thought occurs, a strange little doubt sets in. In fact, we tell ourselves, this evening will be the best—why not?—but also the last like this, this summer. No objective reason for that. Even if we don't live in a region with perfect weather, it won't rain every day. Impossible to imagine a falling-out, envision a catastrophe, even as we cross our fingers.

And so? So, unbelievable as it is, to truly make the most of a summer evening, the idea of its fragility must be at the heart of it, the feeling that we are experiencing this for the last time. I made a fruit salad for dessert. Let's have a cigarette. Let's remember the present. Let's live in the present. With the feeling that it's nearly impossible.

The Time of the Watch Pocket

YOU SEE THEM in old movies. Men of a certain age, often stout, bourgeois, veritable senators of the Third Republic. Between two learned or ribald remarks, they take a gold or silver watch from their watch pocket. The French word for it is *gousset*. Cozy, comfortable, it suggests a satisfied relationship with a projecting abdomen, displayed without shame and caressed without displeasure while inquiring as to the time. There's nothing frenetic in this movement. The watch is proudly wielded, unhurriedly consulted, held at arm's length from the body.

Did these men possess a different kind of time? In any case they didn't feel the need to keep a constant eye on its progress. If they were late, if others were late, their way of registering it could no doubt involve some annoyance, but nothing ate away at their inner nervous systems. They continued to be in command of the operation, carefully sliding the watch back into its little pocket. In three-piece suits, they presided over the course of things.

Guillevic expressed it well: "We possess nothing, ever, except a little time." Poets always speak the truth. And yet . . . When you come across one of those big beautiful watches from the past in a secondhand shop, or inherited from a grandfather, you can't help but think of the vest, the watch chain, of weighing the watch in one hand, this ceremony, this heft. Time did not devour us so when we kept it comfortably in a watch pocket.

Love on the Metro

Y OU'VE SETTLED INTO the small compartment with six seats in the rear of the car. The two of them board at Strasbourg-Saint-Denis, easygoing, in their thirties, backpacks, tennis shoes, short jackets. Sitting down right across from you, they bump into each other, laughing. The brashest one launches in:

—Hey man, not much room here!

His eyes meet yours.

—You've got to be the first one on.

The sentence leaves your mouth with a mocking, conciliatory smile.

Across from you, the expression of the curly blond one changes. He pauses, gauging both your appearance and your tolerance for a little ribbing.

—You must know about that, riding first class in the metro!

Hesitating briefly, you follow with:

—And you, you're old enough to remember when there was such a thing?

Small talk in the guise of banter. In a few minutes, the two pals go back to their private conversation. Then stretching his legs, the curly-haired one looks at you and lapses into intrusive familiarity.

—Did you have a good day?

It could go either way, but something in his eyes belies the presumptuousness. Instead of sending him packing, you feel the sudden desire to unburden yourself, to relinquish the immense fatigue inhabiting you.

—No, a horrible day. I moved both my parents into a retirement home. Into two separate rooms. She's blind and has Alzheimer's. He's exhausted and can hardly walk. And it's my birthday.

Then the masks fall away. In a few seconds and with no noticeable transition, you come to a delicate, compassionate reserve. Unembarrassed, these two, whom you found almost unbearable, reveal themselves to be delightful company, discerning and thoughtful. You confine yourselves to a few well-spaced words. But their eyes are so warm. Everything must be expressed in a few minutes, even your remorse at being wrong at first about this encounter. You don't know when you're going to part ways. They get up at Opéra. Three or four stations, a journey just short and long enough to say to each other I love you.

It's Raining Light

THIS PROVENÇAL TOWN has retained the summer heat. Here, skies have been blue for the past three months. Is it the word *September* at work in your mind, or is it the light mist that has already dissipated by midmorning? Below, in the small marketplace, there are mauve figs arranged in thin balsa wood baskets. On the café terraces, all around, waiters no longer lower the awnings, you no longer seek shade, the sun is gentle, sweet as apricot jam, with a few almonds.

But it's above that this happens, on the blond stone of the town houses, so deceptively austere, so delicately nineteenth century. The tall windows with pale green trim have been opened. Revealing not the secrets of a haughty aristocracy, but rather the voice of a teacher holding class. A whole adolescence is enclosed there, waiting for this to be over, or else to begin, delighting in the texture of new notebooks. Sounds from the market reach the students' ears; their gaze escapes through the two windows and blends that trembling along the edges of the roofs with this first English class. It's just a light wind playing among the branches of the plane trees, dappling the walls with shadow.

In a few days, the senior year curriculum will commence in earnest: contemporary life, the United States. Nevertheless the teacher likes to begin each fall term with this Keats poem:

"To Autumn. Season of mists and mellow fruitfulness."

Here, of course, it's still summer when students return to school. But their gaze is transfixed, everything changes without changing. It's raining light.

Hphh hphh: *Two Small Breaths*

O F COURSE you know that it's very cold. It isn't to prove
it that you expel those puffs of breath. So why? You're
beginning your day—yes, it's always morning when you breathe
this way—and you're feeling both free and frozen. This was no
surprise attack by General Winter. To his unequivocal aggres-
sion you can only respond with the gallant, resolute attitude of
a fighter. Yes, I'm here on the sidewalk, it's freezing and here I
am, I have things to do, I'm alive.

You always breathe twice. Two short exhalations, close
together, tonic. Of course I'm going to take on this whole icy
abstraction of space, don't count on me to melt or freeze. I'm
a tiny power station and look, I'm making smoke. This is an
homage to the adversary. The cold hasn't done things halfway

this morning. But I love challenges. I've stood up to them for so many years. Through this cloud of smoke from my mouth I find my way to school again, that magic of putting a bit of myself into the contours of the landscape, that astonishment, that power. An almost white mist emerges from me, collects for a moment, then dissipates. But the surroundings remain changed by it. Since school days to the present, I vividly exist in those seconds. I salute the cold, the cold salutes my energy. It does not compromise, and neither do I.

In driving rain or biting wind you make yourself smaller, you lie low. But with major cold you keep up your guard. *Hphh hphh*, two short puffs, it's the beginning of the first round, my coach isn't going to throw in the towel. My footwork is lively, I'm free to pace the sidewalk. Soon I'll go into a café, someone will say, "great weather," and everyone at the counter will agree. "Couldn't be better . . ." Yes, it is good, it couldn't be better, it's so much healthier for you. Each of us has privately exhaled our two breaths, no need for witnesses. It's just between you and yourself. Two small breaths. In the arctic air you left your signature.

The Troubled Waters of the Mojito

Y OU CELEBRATE good company gathering outside again, talking without reserve. It's hot, let's have a cocktail. It's often a matter of tropical colors and flavors, coconut, shades of red reminiscent of Club Med sunshine, to be drunk half-seriously, making fun of your thirst and childish taste for sweets, about to be creolized by rum.

And then there's the mojito. The name sounds South American. But something entirely unexpected awaits you. However hard you try to keep following the conversation, to feign indifference, when the waiter places your drink on the table, you feel an adventure about to begin.

It's so perverse, so murky. An immediate invitation to dive, to plumb ocean depths difficult to master. You'll swim in search of wreckage maybe, or strange seaweed that means to trap or caress you. It's the ambiguity that's tempting.

The mojito is simultaneously opaque and transparent. There are greens of course, but also darker zones, with more clarity near the surface and unfathomable mysteries below—until you have to come up for air. You take a sip, surprised at this coolness that evokes the charms of a damp lagoon. Any cocktail demands to be consumed slowly, punctuated with pauses, neglect and return. With a mojito, you don't call the shots. Tasting becomes a fascination and the cocktail takes command. The most surprising thing is how its sweetness persists through a mangrove swamp of noxious flavors. You let its cold fever penetrate you, you abandon yourself. When this glaucous drifting ends, you know heat and euphoria will follow. But you have to wander the mint leaf forest, tame your fear of being engulfed, abandon all hope of light. Swim through the transgressions, get lost, founder, endlessly search, descend to the bottom. All of which gives rise to the pleasure.

Public Orgasm

I T'S OFTEN at the mention of a simple sweet. Very pure, natural, and rather old-fashioned: real French toast, chocolate mousse, but true, authentic mousse, fresh raspberries drenched in cream. Then it's stronger than they are. Just the idea and they close their eyes, tilt back their heads, arching delightedly as they let out an almost guttural *mmmm*, coming from the very depths of the most irrepressible pleasure.

The ones who dare to dramatize this ineffable ecstasy to the point of practically fainting are nearly always attractive and diaphanously thin. They are the same ones who turn down almost everything at the dinner table, refuse second helpings with a weary smile, develop clever strategies for keeping their quasi-anorexia both hidden and well mannered. They are not to be outdone. They pick at their food like birds, but can make clear in a few seconds of simulated bliss their superiority in the area least expected of them: gourmandism.

You have to admit there's a certain something to their pantomime, and even more: a sensuality that their perfect elegance takes to the very edge of sexuality. Despite all the consensual perfection of the scene, you feel, according to your role, a little uncomfortable, a little disturbed. And then very quickly, and almost out of revenge, you start wondering. Aren't these part-time sybarites a bit out of touch? If their public orgasms can take on such dimensions, does that suggest volcanic fireworks when they abandon themselves in private? It's reassuring to convince yourself that's not at all the case. Yes, without a doubt, their best lover, male or female, is just the idea of chocolate mousse.

Eyelids of Oblivion

YOU DO THIS when you wear glasses. You raise them with just the thumb and forefinger, which come to massage the area below the closed eyelids. Most often you do this alone, and never when you're talking. The thumb and forefinger seem out of proportion, almost antagonistic, one a burly worker, the other threatening or reflexive, but they slide over the closed eyes with symmetrical insistence, from the outer edge to the bridge of the nose. Does this answer some physiological need? Not really. Rather it's a kind of calming retreat, as if to free oneself from immense weariness. Head bent forward, you repeat the operation three or four times.

Glasses don't really cooperate in this maneuver. They go all askew—and it's always the index finger that pushes them higher. There's something appealing in the posture: it's easy to imagine an office scene in an old black-and-white Hollywood murder mystery. The eyelids aren't closed as on the beach, where they're lowered just enough to take in thousands of protozoa. Here, they close heavily, in defiance of protocol, the pressure of the fingers only confirming this desire to escape. From what? From everything, the stress of 5 p.m., the night that's coming on, the inescapability of a fate you didn't choose, you hardly questioned, you've just abolished for a few seconds in this momentary refusal of a crushing task. You dispel the exhaustion by underlining it. And it's done, already you're coming back. Just before opening your eyes, you reposition your glasses, thumb and middle finger spanning the far ends of the frames. You return to the struggle of the present.

Memory of Forgetting

S HE'S BEEN in this Alzheimer's unit of the retirement home for a few days. There's a code required for leaving. She can't escape. She doesn't want to escape. She's blind. The first night must have been horrible. Trying over and over to feel her way along the walls. Humiliating details of course. During the day things are a little better. A caregiver offers her an arm to walk endlessly up and down the hall. Her legs are still good. The nurse says:

—It's going fine, she's sweet. A little agitated today. I'll leave you two to yourselves.

And then more loudly, turning toward her:

—You have a visitor!

Yes, a little agitated. More like total anguish. She says she's lost, that she no longer recognizes anything. She asks:

—And you, who are you?

You tell her that her husband is here, in another room.

—I have a husband?

—Yes, a husband who loves you very much. You lived together for a very long time. There are photos of you in his room, he looks at them often.

—Oh, he has photos of me? Do you think I'll be able to visit him?

—Yes, I'll take you to him. You can listen to music together in the afternoon.

She knows what it is to have a husband. She knows what it is to be loved. She knows what it is to have photos. She's happy to come sit beside this man who, five minutes earlier, she wasn't the least bit aware of. She hums along with the Schubert impromptu and you're amazed at her incredible memory for melodies, for songs.

Her face has relaxed and become almost radiant, ecstatic. For someone doing so badly, how can she still be so well? Why must she suffer that same anguish in her room again tonight? She'll remember that she lost something, she won't know what. They say it's hell. But there isn't a word for it.

Immobile Polka

—Y<small>OU CAN</small> hold him, if you want to!

You always want to. Taking a baby in one's arms is a privilege, a proof of trust that you want only to confirm. You're surprised to find how well you've inwardly retained the shape of the cradle, one arm raised a bit to support the neck, the other below it, enveloping the feet, the lower part of the body so light. It's good, this sensation of instantly giving warmth and protection, of experiencing physically the power to pacify.

If the baby starts crying, you'll quickly hand him over, saying no, it's fine, of course he prefers his mama. But even so, there are stakes. Is it to ward off that risk that you immediately begin this slight bouncing of the whole body? Not at all frenetic, but you bob from side to side, almost automatically and with paradoxical vigor, as if it were urgent to instill the idea of gentleness, to elicit a smile, to induce blessed sleep. Seen from the outside, this attempt to win favor can seem rough, unnatural. Bent forward, you ask your legs for a springing motion that rises all the way to the shoulders. It's like some kind of strenuous physical labor, as though you had to reproduce the rolling of a boat, the bumping of a car, the pitching of a train—all the rhythms of those modes of transportation that can put babies to sleep. Wanting to give that peace while remaining in place, you abandon yourself to an affable, vertical dance, a little ridiculous, but you don't care. You're holding infancy against you, in the hollow of you. You're celebrating it as best you can, with an awkward polka that never leaves its spot.

I Really Like This Place!

THIS SUNLIT MORNING in early winter is off to a good start. They run toward you at your meeting place, parkas and ski masks, rosy cheeks, sparkling eyes. It's the first time you're taking them to the children's book room in Montreuil. The older one already knows how to read. But at four years old, the younger one is only in his second year of preschool. Since summer he has been drawing letters on blank sheets of paper, meticulously, with great concentration. He gathers them together and then asks what he has written. At first that made him laugh, imaginary words he'd traced without knowing it. But now, it seems to you, he doesn't find it so funny and although he doesn't admit it, he has that burning desire to read like his brother, spelling out the world instead of inventing it.

It doesn't matter. You've told him there are so many magical books at the Salon de Montreuil, comic books with almost no text where only the pictures really count, fold-out books, plus shows to watch, story tellers. He has a little backpack with sausage sandwiches and a water bottle.

Riding the metro, he's less talkative than usual, exchanging excited looks with you from time to time. You give him a hand sign: four more stations!

And there you are. Getting off at Robespierre. He climbs the stairs with the vigor of a mountaineer. At the top the vaulted ceiling opens onto an almost postwar landscape. Just ahead, a section of blackened wall between filthy, burned-out apartment buildings. He must be the first one ever to exclaim here, with a beaming smile, "I really like this place!"

Vendor for a Day

REALLY, YOU DON'T envy them. At big antique and second-hand fairs, the vendors look bored. You know it's part of their strategy of course. If they appear to have no interest in selling, that's supposed to make you want to buy. You imagine their best moments are the lunch breaks with colleagues, amid Louis XVI furniture and Persian rugs, pulling up chairs, sausage and a glass of wine, trading anecdotes, hey guess what, Patrick got taken by Michel.

No, what's good is to have your own stand once a year at the tag sale in your neighborhood or village.

Relationships between humans are funny. It's such a fine line. People you know by sight, you've crossed paths, you've never spoken. And there, all of a sudden, through the mediation of an object, book, painting, lamp, or toy, it becomes easy. At first you stick with simple shop talk, oh yeah, that crane works, it just needs batteries. That's the key. Each of you earns the right to drop the usual propriety and shyness that inhibit you. Not that you bare your soul. Nevertheless you find it easy to recall times with the children, to remark how life has changed. One thing leads to another and you discover acquaintances you have in common. If it's getting toward evening, you propose a glass of rosé. Accepting involves no commitment. This is a tag sale. A world apart, where a laid-back philosophy that you thought had disappeared survives. An oasis. You wish it could be like this all year long, but one day each year, that's pretty good too.

Flesh and Cloth

A WOMAN OF a certain age. She wears dresses, floral prints. She practices that sort of outdated elegance that makes Sempé's little gentlemen exclaim, "But where do they hide in winter, all these charming women who return to us in spring?" On the sidewalk in front of the shop, she notices the sales rack and its row of summer dresses with reasonable necklines, repeated leafy motifs, classic toile de Jouy style.

She stops. She's tempted of course, but she isn't a pushover. In this little game of good deals and desire, she's anxious to maintain her reserve, her sense of aesthetics and wise spending. So she leans forward and her hand reaches for the hem of the dress. Why? Undoubtedly because it's only there she can gather enough fabric to truly judge its texture. All cotton, or a synthetic blend? Light or warm? Wrinkle-free or not? A little frown accompanies this examination. It conveys the seriousness of the ritual. The woman feels the cloth between her fingers. Gently, so as not to incur reproach. Afterwards of course, she'll consider the lines of the dress, the cut, the chances that it will work for her, will correspond to her style, or allow her to adapt it ever so slightly. She may ask to try it on.

But her first contact is the most visceral. With her flesh, she apprehends the material. For all its apparent austerity, there's sensual pleasure in the rubbing of fabric against fingers. A long history of female knowledge encourages and justifies it. To go from indifferent hesitation to satisfied desire, this ceremony at the base of the hem is required, this way of getting to the bottom of things. Between thumb and forefinger, the caressed cloth can no longer pretend to be what it's not. The potential for elegance must have the backing of truth.

The Gestures of San Giacomo

THERE ARE FOUNTAINS almost everywhere on the piazzas of Venice, but the one at Campo San Giacomo da l'Orio will always be unique. Possibly because it's nestled between two flaking red benches that form a wide angle, and probably because it abuts two small gardens where school children have planted flower beds in the shade of plane trees. It calls for a certain abandon, rituals for decanting its coolness. The most common posture of course is the one with two hands joined to form a cup before drinking. But more often than elsewhere, drinkers don't mind jumping back to dodge the water splashing on the flat stone. Forget elegance, you take it easy here, you make yourself at home. Sometimes a young woman slips off her sandals and offers her legs, one at a time, to the spray of water. She's wearing shorts or else she lifts her skirt high above her knees, especially when she leans down to rinse off the dust from her walk, her fingertips moving slowly toward her ankles. Then a familiar silhouette appears, a late eighteenth- or early nineteenth-century painting, a slightly dated femininity reinvented in the outflowing of the present.

Often there's a line at the San Giacomo fountain. But there's never a feeling of waiting, not the least impatience. There's no hurry, and it's summer. Charmed tourists, plastic water bottles in hand, know that they have to earn that water, then savor it leisurely along the narrow streets after having dampened cheeks and forehead.

The children who were drawing with colored chalk on the piazza reluctantly abandon their artistic postures, some stretched almost flat on their bellies, others on their knees. They come to wash their hands, all the while keeping an eye on their work. Maybe it's time for their afternoon snack, or maybe not. These gestures succeed one another, different and alike, softened, ennobled by the gentleness of the water, the perfection of the fountain in the shade of San Giacomo.

En Route Virtuosos

IN THE WAITING area, they've installed a piano. There's one in each of the big Paris railway stations now, but you never know how that will go. In the Gare du Nord the other day, an older woman set her suitcase down beside her and then played, with great application, *Jesu, Joy of Man's Desiring* before melting back into the crowd, aware that no one had stopped to listen. She left without looking around, suitcase in hand, a little smile on her lips, of annoyance or contentment.

At Saint-Lazare, the level of playing is consistently high, in a wide variety of registers. Passersby interrupt their journeys for a few minutes and thus create an ever-replenished circle. Nothing at all like the line for burgers.

Pianists of all ages. While one plays, two or three others wait, standing near the instrument or leaning on the railing. They show no impatience, nod their heads to a ragtime rhythm, offer an approving smile to the virtuosic sweep of a Chopin waltz, acknowledge with an air of complicity the jazzed-up version of a film theme.

It's nice, this courteous association of players who follow one after the other, exchanging a friendly word as they take the bench, sharing the exultation and the vanished dreams—life.

It's all very delicately civilized, how the pianists wait. They know that their turn will come—it will be decided intuitively, about fifteen minutes to perform, they can play again afterwards if they have the time. They have the time.

They almost succeeded in their profession; they could have, all they needed was a bit of luck, something distinctive about their talent, the chance to work. It's strange. The waiting area seems to float, suspended. If you listen long enough, you see what you haven't seen, the restored stained-glass windows in brown tones along the upper walls: Rouen, Le Havre, Dieppe, Deauville. You see all the pleasure of the pianists at ease before their keyboard, playing for a faithless audience—who, in the onrush of commuters, nonetheless stopped. And those stolen seconds are beautiful.

Running Your Hand Over a Book

SOMEONE HAS JUST given you this book. In essence it holds a promise of solitude, retreat, silence. But for the moment you're talking about it: yes, I've wanted to read it, no I haven't read it, I liked the last one a lot, the bestseller from five or six years ago a little less so... The book rests on your thigh. Almost unconsciously you run your hand over the back cover. Beyond the conventional exchange that continues, you feel a kind of calming. This is a volume that you can touch, that you experience below the surface.

It's curious. The small talk surrounding the object goes on, very agreeably and mutually, but the delight of your hand's contact transports you far away, despite the apparent propriety of the scene. The book is cool and warm at the same time, smooth as the perfection of another world. Of course the person who gave it to you loves reading as much as you do. And she's no more fooled by these moments than you are, as she recites her own lines in turn: I really liked it, it's one of those books that you don't want to finish, for a long time I saved the last three pages . . .

But under this sincere exchange floats a kind of necessary and reciprocal hypocrisy. The value of this object—its emotional and market value—must remain ambiguous. We both know that the book is meant to go beyond our lives, our rituals, the evenings we share. I run my hand over its cover. It's not completely mine yet. Without looking, I can touch and sense: already it's the book that possesses me.

The Ostentatious After-You

THE SIDEWALK IS neither wide nor narrow. Two can easily walk there, even if the grocer's stand juts out a bit. But nevertheless. Seeing her approach, you sense it immediately: the person you're about to pass is going to stop, execute a withdrawal, and back up against the wall into the corner with the orange crates. After all, if this maneuver were really necessary, you could certainly have initiated it yourself, you aren't so boorish as all that. But the scenario offers no recourse: you're now indebted for a favor you didn't request, that serves absolutely no purpose. It's a low blow. Hardly moving your lips, unsmiling, you mouth a very polite thank-you, into which you slip an ounce of reprobation—your slightly raised eyebrows counter: "No need for this, but thanks just the same."

You've had time to see whom you're dealing with. A person brought up very well. Too well. A person who hasn't turned her good manners into an unconscious asset, but rather an offensive display. An odd attack, which takes on the appearance of a humble retreat, yet without concealing this silent jubilation in proving oneself to be more courteous, more considerate, more civilized.

The one to whom you're beholden hasn't chosen her victim randomly. She doesn't display her good breeding for the most oblivious passersby, those glued to the screens of their smartphones, or wearing headphones, singing to themselves. No, clearly she's seen that you're not so far removed from her own moral and social universe. She knows that you're offended. You're forced to advance: she steps aside, she has won.

Tango on the Seine

Q UAI MONTEBELLO, summer evenings, when you've remained sitting cross-legged long after the picnic to watch the sun go down between the towers of Notre-Dame, you think to yourself that the best is already over. Nevertheless indistinct wafts of music convince you to wander further east, toward Tino Rossi Square. A circle of light stands out against the blue of night and you hear Latin accents and rhythms. Yes, there below, they're dancing the tango.

What immediately captivates you is how serious this is. Earnest faces, or tense with effort, but all equally concentrated, as if there were something at stake, a desire to meet the challenge. It's only afterwards that you begin to decipher the body language. Clearly this is no simple feat. Following the accordion's sinewy languor and reprises, couples glide in sophisticated undulations without a glance toward their partners. Without the slightest nod toward neighboring couples, despite the great number of them. Are they equipped with radar like bats? Undulating like fish without a single collision, hardly brushing against one another. The fish bowl maintains its magic fluidity. Even a minor accident would apparently profane this temple dedicated to the Tango god.

Each with an arm held out before them, hand in hand, the dancers submit to a ritual of sublimated eroticism. Because below, hips sway, legs intersect with a complexity that doesn't at all dispel the audacity of the movement. Often a young woman dances with an older partner. Males are rare and for the most part middle-aged. But drama is no less present, the codified embrace no less passionate, lust may even be heightened by so much restraint—as if scrupulous respect for the dance steps keeps one from falling headlong into the flames.

Wind blows from the Seine, a little cooler. It's surprising. Having just escaped a consuming passion, the dancers thank each other and politely take their leave. At the square named for Tino Rossi, his Marinella drifts away, disappears into Paris's Argentinian night.

Washing the Windows

YOU DECIDE TO do it because it's a beautiful day. You're amazed at the quality of light even at dawn, but there's no denying how ruthlessly the light reveals long dusty streaks on the window panes. Have you really been living in such an opaque prison? As a rule, unexpected household chores hardly inspire enthusiasm. But washing the windows is another thing altogether. Of course there's the immediate shame that sets in, but that quickly lifts and gives way to an almost triumphant jubilation. When you vacuum and re-vacuum the house, you bow your head, you submit. Washing the windows involves entirely different movements. You open up, you breathe, your whole face takes in the sun. In the past you let yourself be talked into using a special product, icy blue and oily, that took forever to rinse off. From now on, no more cleaning aids. Everything must be done with hot water, immaculate paper towel, in full transparency.

It's a brisk exhilaration. The glass is so unyielding, it resists the energy expended. You've met your match and this is certainly no sinecure. You thought you'd cleaned both sides of the panes; opening the window reveals marks, a dull reflection, a persistent indistinct haze in one corner. Sometimes a few small rings of dried white paint require scratching off with the edge of your fingernail. It's then you approach the true essence, even while you remain cautiously humble. And really, it's not so bad to have prolonged this operation. Certain domestic tasks still retain slightly derogatory connotations. But washing the windows? It celebrates the wedding of inside and out, overcomes a bit of dullness in a dazzling day.

Driving a Shopping Cart

A SHOPPING CART IS both docile and stubborn. Its wide wheelbase, its ample proportions call for easy and abundant consumption. Jars, cans, and bottles ask only to leave their shelves to dive into this belly-on-wheels, a vaguely obscene outgrowth, metaphor for a very public open encounter between planned and impromptu desire. Of course you made a list, and you're sticking to it, in the sense that all the anticipated articles will come to occupy this ambulatory basket and be checked off. But that mental satisfaction won't keep you from succumbing to the sale on Provençal rosés, the amazing opportunity to get three goat cheeses for the price of two, the enticing display of oh so Scottish whisky—buy one bottle and you take possession of them all.

This is done a step at a time, with a feeling of perfect free will. Why disdain the handlebar for directing the cart? Because pushing like that, hands close together, shoulders hunched, seems to subject you to an unpleasant servitude. No, you're not the plaything of strategies organized at your expense. You seize the far corners of basket, you freely survey the aisles, you walk tall.

You have nothing but pity for the domestic amazon who passes you. Her frenzy to fulfill her shopping mission seems like a reproach—not a wasted glance, no hesitation, like a bee for its hive. Ruthless, she goes straight to the essentials—and further reinforces your delightful sense of being the flaneur.

For your part, you steer your cart as you please. That's how you view your errant course at least, until the moment when you have to turn too sharply. Then the shopping cart's true personality comes to light: it has a rebellious nature. It suddenly resists, stiffens, then freezes. You glance at the wheels, no sign of rust. It's a question of the shopping cart's philosophy: it doesn't like to turn. It's designed to cruise the whole length of the aisle, to make your mouth water without omission, without remission. You think you're driving it, but in fact, it's driving you.

The Third Balcony

—N o, I'm sorry, it's sold out. Or wait. . .

You knew it. It's so hard to get seats to marvel at Michel Bouquet in *Le roi se meurt*. But there are those ellipses in the voice. . .

—Possibly, December 22, I might have two single seats in the third balcony. But I should warn you: it's very cramped!

On December 22 you confirm that. It is very cramped. You have a hard time sliding your legs in sideways against the guardrail. You're on the edge of the void where the slightest glance down to the audience in the orchestra results in vertigo. The railing doesn't seem high enough. Of course the theater is Italianate in style, but on a very reduced scale and very perpendicular. So close to the roof, you feel cut off from the reality of the place, marginalized. Below there's activity, loud conversation, bustle. No one looks up to observe the exiles in the third balcony.

But when the lights go down, your isolation suddenly becomes delightful. Almost uncanny. This doesn't seem at all like attending a play. That tiny head straight beneath you, is it really Michel Bouquet's? Hard to connect it with the face you've seen in films: that distinctive chin, those thin lips, bright eyes. In a few minutes, you begin to feel privileged to get so much distance on the idea of Michel Bouquet. If you were sitting in the orchestra, you'd have a comfortable view of him, but Ionesco's text would get mixed up with your memories of the actor. His stillness as the Ionescian king would merge with all his animation in *La femme infidèle* or *Le promeneur du Champ-de-Mars*, with the discomfort this actor instills in his roles—that disturbing perverse old bachelor side of him, mopping his brow with a handkerchief after a bad sweat.

Nothing of that from the third balcony. You have only a bird's-eye view of Michel Bouquet, his quintessence. Listening carefully, you recognize that voice, now concentrated in the character. At the bottom of the well, a kind of alchemy is taking place. Impossible not to think how lucky you are to be seeing Michel Bouquet's *Le roi se meurt*, since you came so close to not seeing it at all, or to seeing something else. You have to crouch down, lean forward, focus, make an effort, for which, in return, you experience a bubble of pure theater, free of all contingent social rituals, all the bourgeoisie. You think of Roland Barthes's line: "In every tragedy by Racine, it's a question of a fleet in a port, as though to attest that its negation is near." *Le roi se meurt* that you almost didn't see, that you see differently, that you see badly, is heightened, powerful. Life should be lived from the third balcony.

Wringing Red Currants

T HIS IS A forgotten gesture, I believe. I love it because it is powerful, and a bit disturbing. It brings into play two figures, both dead: my grandmother and my mother. They are officiating in the kitchen, sleeves rolled up, standing, slightly bent, over a basin. They are wringing a white cotton cloth full of red currants. The juice runs out quickly, then slows down, but the torsion intensifies at the two ends, mercilessly: all the juice must be expressed. The muslin has become darker than the fruit, with a complete nimbus of mauve. A slight feeling of disgust hovers over the operation. These two women whom I love, these two strong and gentle women, don't speak to each other, intent on the violence of their effort.

It's strange. This is the first stage of making red currant jelly.

Next will follow cooking it in the kettle, pouring it into jars, its sunlit, comforting red soon sealed with a light disc of paraffin. At the end will come a sweet serenity, with just a touch of tartness recalling the transgression of eating red currants by the handful in the garden. But before that pleasure, there must be this ritual, vaguely barbaric because of the secret connotations between white cloth and blood red fruit?

Those two women so close to me took on a singular energy. The summer heat made them sweat. It's as though they were condemned to a kind of cruel and necessary fierceness, a base posture, a heavy and viscous femininity. How could that bloody rite, their convulsive gesture, have led them to the transparent stillness of the jelly?

Apart Together

YOU MADE LOVE. You might say that you're still in the midst of making love. But no. Your hand seeks the other's shoulder and rests there in a different way. You've just come together almost as one. It seems that you're still immersed in that pleasure, and yet you're already so quiet, so composed. It's good to feel the difference in this gesture even before a single word is spoken. Good to feel that, without rupture, an old and tender camaraderie reestablishes itself almost immediately. You thought you had crossed the line, always this feeling of exceeding the bounds, without which love would be nothing. And there you are, beyond the frontier, in that country both new and familiar.

You take each other by the shoulder, you draw close, you

catch your breath. There's the slightest hesitancy, a curious intimidation, just following so much license. Whatever time has passed, it's still new. It's as though, between your confidence in taking risks and your confidence in reconnecting afterwards, there's a bridge to cross. In the end, this may be the most difficult gesture of all, because appearances don't lie: you haven't reached exactly the same understanding; that would be too easy, there would be no more desire. It's that moment when the shoulder's sense of security doesn't necessarily come from the one embracing or the one embraced. You're two at risk, you risk the silence, the amazement of two inviolate trusts, when there was so much you wanted to lay bare. You're familiar but you're changed as well, otherwise the game wouldn't be worth the stakes. Maybe you'll say something stupid. In a minute or two, not yet. A hand rests on a shoulder. You're together, apart.

A Key Case and Crepes

I T BELONGED TO someone you loved, who died a year ago.
A beige leather key case with a button snap. An object that
must have seemed modern in the early sixties, but he'd kept it
until the end of his life. He slid it into the pocket of his raincoat
or his pants. Practical for flat keys: the house key, the key to
the mailbox, the garage. He undid the snap with the end of his
thumb. An angled flap of leather opened to reveal, along the
top edge, a small gold bar pierced with little holes where the
keys were attached. When you used one, the other two leapt
out with it.

That's the gesture. That movement of the wrist to flip the
keys back into place, with a tiny recoil, a bit like when you
toss a crepe in a pan. He did it while he talked, it was no great

feat. But even so. A certain deftness, a touch of agility, almost casual. At the beginning of a shared walk or going to do errands in town. The simplest of good times lying ahead. This modest sleight of hand was part of the unspoken pleasure of being together, of the day's good cheer.

And then, just like that. No more shared errands. Among the objects of his that you kept, you might not have imagined adopting this key case, completely outdated, inseparable from a type of pants, a type of raincoat. But the other day you opened the mailbox and the keys again performed their gymnastic escape. Then, a smile rose to your lips as you tried the wrist move for tossing crepes. So good to rediscover that lost companionship in the guise of a solitary gesture! So great to be together again, ready to share the day. The day before, the day after. In the retraction of the wrist, the invincible present that holds everything, even the comforting vigor of an outmoded key case.

Alone!

Y OU HAVE TO admit it, you're not in the best of moods. All day there's been one annoyance after another. Nevertheless, you know that tonight you have to go to the Olympia to see that singer you like so much—well, actually, you admire five or six of his songs.

It's hard to believe, but the show's hardly begun and while you thought you'd feel an immediate rapport with him, you find this guy unbearable. Long-winded, so irritating with his introductions. "This is a song that came to me one rainy day, looking out the window onto the street." Followed by lots of biographical detail, a whole little history lacking any real excitement, and in conclusion: "It's called . . ." And the singer's voice adopts an ostentatious indifference as he reveals the title of his best-known hit.

The audience, that spineless creature, that glutton for punishment, reacts with expected enthusiasm. So now you find the crowd servile and the singer a snob. You feel like you've fallen into a stifling pit. Hard to keep clapping, even with just your fingertips. And it takes a certain bad faith to sit there, stoking your exasperation over both the toad and his toadies.

And then in a flash it hits you. After all, why not escape at intermission? And that's what you do, with a smile on your lips. Outside, you take a deep breath, you go get a beer. It's marvelous. You've never felt this free, this light. What a joy not to have to share in such predictable zeal! Here outside, passersby are so likable, so different from the fans crammed into the music hall, having checked all critical thinking at the door. It's like when you were a child and you'd just reported a bad grade to your parents. Relieved, released, you're floating on air. And the evening's still young. You take off to wander about Paris, while, back at the Olympia, they have to keep applauding. How great to be alone!

Munching a Turnip

I<small>T'S NEVER PREMEDITATED</small>. You don't say to yourself: "Okay, I'm going to get a turnip from the refrigerator and peel it so I can eat it raw." First of all, munching a turnip involves theft. The peeled vegetables in the colander by the sink are an image of perfection! Leeks, potatoes, carrots, turnips: they've all left the earth behind, lost all but their least perceptible desquamations. They're naked, radiant, tonic, like new babies. You still remember sinking your teeth into a raw potato, and the unpleasant sensation of it, all chalky and bitter. Same for the cardboard tartness of leek stalks. Your desire focuses on the only two possible prey: carrots and turnips. A peeled carrot is very tempting, not simply orange, rather a mellow, almost coral tone. Cut lengthwise, it reveals borders, flamelike structures.

Maybe a little too hard for the incisor. Then too, you can chomp it down without remorse, there will always be enough carrots. And that's why you prefer the turnip.

It's forever the poor relative, reduced to a few precious, endangered specimens. Mauve at the crown, there's something a little quaint and pudgy about it, ideally conceived for the idea of soup. Passing through the trial of the vegetable peeler, it attains an immaculate whiteness. How could such a polished stone taste like anything? But that's the privilege of a raw turnip. It has an ideal texture, just enough give to heighten the crunch. Useless to probe its taste for any hint of its cooked siblings, sometimes almost sickeningly bland, tender to the point of dissolving, and a kind of dirty beige. The raw turnip releases in the mouth a slightly smoky aroma, a touch of hazelnut, a secret something that seems to contradict its consistency.

You won't be able to confirm its singular gifts. Impossible to steal a second turnip, the theft would become too obvious. You can't fill up on them. A turnip can be spirited away during off hours when the kitchen tolerates light fingers. But don't come back. It's a pleasure to be taken on the sly.

Time is a Beach

YOU OFTEN GO to the seashore. But beach is a state of mind. It could be beside a lake, a stream, a river. The choice is rarely without context. It'll be based on old familial roots here, a welcoming aunt, an organizing cousin there, or simply an internal predilection for the sea, the mountains, or the countryside. Internal. Despite outward appearances, it's really your inner depths that you'll return to. It won't be a matter of "doing" Patagonia or Kenya.

No, summer vacations, real vacations, are both less costly and more serious. You aren't seeking new sensations, but rather a lost freedom, something of the lightheartedness bound up with the rites of childhood. Time is no longer punctuated by deadening reports on daily news shows, but rather by the single question that matters: will it be nice tomorrow? The sun should be out, its heat gentle, relaxing—you deserve that. And you'll be looking for water, of course. The reverberation of words over water and the crash of diving in are the two sounds of summer vacation. And soon rising in counterpoint, a grandmother's exclamation: "Not so far Mattéo, I want to see you!" But even this worry is close to pleasure. First thing and last, you plumb the water's depths, marveling at how you desire its coolness. You fish, or splash in the waves, search for prawn or roach, build dams. Or you do nothing, you watch others scurry about.

Sometimes too, and as though in necessary contrast, there must be a day of rain, a bit of boredom, shopping, excursions to aquariums, cheese shops. "Points of interest" that are never really interesting.

Because what you want is the immobility, to rediscover the sun, to let life slow down. There's something humbling about this way of enjoying oneself, in close proximity to others and almost with them. You're part of the same family, the family that takes multigenerational vacations. You put off meals, a little shade for a midday picnic, and, well after aperitifs, that delicious exasperation over dinner.

And are you happier? Well yes, of course, maybe. You have time to ask yourself that question. Sisyphus stops rolling his stone. And then you have time to dispel it, like that small cloud that was hiding the sun and is beginning to clear; you'll still have a lovely evening. You just have to put on a sweater, make friends with eternity.

You Rise

YOU LOVE this show. You've laughed a lot, and from the very first, with a feeling of being alone. Before the curtain rose, you had sized up the audience a bit. Older, provincial, rather bourgeois. Season-ticket holders, many of them. They were recalling last week's play with that disinterest that speaks more of social ease than cultural enthusiasm. Here, audiences remain circumspect, don't get swept up in Paris trends.

This consummate art of reserve will be practiced shamelessly throughout the evening. The most hilarious lines will produce only a discreet murmur, sometimes following a brief pause that eventually raises your doubts about the audience's comprehension. It's difficult not to feel uncomfortable for the actors. No doubt they're accustomed to variations in audience reaction time when they perform, but more than once you feel them getting slightly thrown off, no longer able to rely on what they thought would be big moments. You're hoping for a little remorse from the crowd when the time comes to applaud. But you're counting more on the deferred pleasure of sharing with those who weren't there all they missed. You clap very hard, you shout bravo—at least let the cast come back on stage for a respectable number of curtain calls. Will you press your enthusiasm to the point of trying for a standing ovation? Given the ambient listlessness, that seems pure provocation. You risk finding yourself all alone, ridiculous. At the same time, it doesn't take much to prompt herd behavior. You glance around quickly at your fellow spectators. They remain seated, hopelessly stuck to their chairs. Alright, it's a question of honor, you have to act on your convictions—too bad if it looks like a reproach to the others for their apathy. You rise. For just a moment, you believe you possess the mad power to change the course of destiny. Didn't you sense some rustling to your right?

Your neighbor has just stood up. But he's not applauding. He's taking advantage of your uprising to slip on his coat and dash out as quickly as possible. The last bitter dregs.

Folded Album Cover

ADOLESCENCE. Alone in your room. The sixties, the great age of vinyl. You put the record on the turntable, you took the album cover, you stretched out on your bed, legs drawn up. You didn't linger over the front, which was almost always a close-up frontal shot of the singer's face, the gaze too intimate, the name too large. On the back were listed all the song titles, information regarding the studio, mixing, arrangements. But the moment that mattered was when you opened the fold, when you multiplied the surface area by two. Inside on the double panel, you discovered the large photo. You rested it on your thighs. It was heavy cardboard and never lay completely flat. The angle at which it opened was important: you were penetrating a universe, but you were also taking it into yourself, you were giving it a kind of spatial dimension, in keeping with the song, the materiality of the sound. Often in black and white, the photo inside truly revealed something. Sometimes it was taken in the singer's house or garden. You weren't necessarily looking to invade their privacy. You also liked it when the setting has been carefully selected: Jean Ferrat bounding across flat rocks in an Ardèche stream, Simon and Garfunkel against a fence in Central Park, Jacques Brel walking along a Belgian beach. You remained there, you inhabited the image, without fail.

Later there were cassettes, then CDs. At first, you thought how great that would be, a whole little book slipped into the CD case. In miniature, it would engender an even more beautiful, even more cherished impression. But you have to admit it: you never really spent time with those little books, you never embarked, as you did sitting on your bed opening the album cover. And now the idea of the disc has almost vanished. We listen to songs superimposed on life; that's something else altogether. In the subway, on the sidewalks, many wear expressions of delight, caught up in the rhythm or the ideas. Many smile, as though they're smiling to themselves. At the same time, some are returning to vinyl; it seems that it's cool again. The folded album cover may well make a comeback—along with folding up your knees to listen on your bed.

An Opera for Nothing Much

IMMEDIATELY YOU FEEL you're about to witness a great performance. She has a little time, and more importantly, a little space. The train is nearly empty: she was able to claim for herself an area meant for four passengers. She isn't particularly flamboyant, hardly a flirt. Entering the car, she didn't seem to turn any heads. She consulted her smartphone: a short pause, the hint of a smile, then she slid it into her bag.

And now, here it comes. It's as if you knew the whole scenario in advance. She reaches her arms into the air and feels for a clip above the nape of her neck. But to let loose this avalanche of hair requires a swaying of the head from side to side, soon accompanied by a movement of the shoulders. And then, is that an expression of slightly bored exhaustion crossing her face, is this the full extent of the onslaught? There's a whole indisputable realm, an essential femininity that she could legitimately claim as hers and that strangely seems to elude her. While she claims its opulence, her hair suddenly appears possessed by a life of its own, which takes command.

The stakes are high. Will she have her way with it? After a few deliciously libertarian shakes, her mane seems to submit for the moment. The play of her hands, her arms, reveals a consummate mastery. And she's in no hurry. She wants time to imagine all her possibilities, all the different women that these hairstyles, abandoned even as they appear, parade past in a matter of minutes. There are unexpected arrangements, a few surprises revealed intentionally, others half-consciously, and there's time travel as well: for an instant she seems medieval, far away in her tower. A second later, she's jazzing it up in Saint-Germain-des-Prés.

Although clearly there's something a bit strange about this: an imperceptible slide toward resignation, disappointment. Because they're are so fleeting? All of those intermediate phases seem preferable to what you sense she's about to become again.

In fact, you're surprised that those flowing streams, those voluptuous waves, were so determined to end in this little bun, practical, you imagine, but curiously stunted, as though antithetical to the lushness abolished in obtaining it. She signs off on the knot without a flourish, no bow, no curtain call. All that for just that!

The Locks are Gold

A<small>T FIRST</small> you smiled. A few padlocks here and there along the parapet of Pont des Arts. Initials and the date either engraved or written with indelible marker on the metal. A romantic idea that seemed original. Fixed into the iron, onto the steel, a promise of eternal attachment. Over the Seine, which forever flows, far from Pont Mirabeau and Apollinaire's melancholy. In the light of Paris, where passersby endlessly pass. You looked without looking, you looked at the idea, you smiled.

Then after a few years, padlocks had overrun the place. On Pont des Arts, hardly any space was left. You began to see them on Pont Simone-de-Beauvoir, on Pont de l'Archevêché. At the ends of the bridges, street peddlers had set up shop. It was no longer a matter of making public both a declaration and a secret, but of copying others.

And soon the alarm was sounded. All that steel was much too heavy, over a hundred tons. Some sections of metal fencing collapsed. So along Pont des Arts, they said STOP. Along Pont de l'Archevêché, the parapet is now smothered.

Nevertheless, when the sun plays across the metal, these love locks are beautiful. All the contiguous messages form a golden gate, an arch over the river. Paris is not complaining. Paris is the philosopher's stone. After five or six years, many of these relationships have no doubt dissolved. But it's good like this, the trace of them remaining in the hum from the riverfront drives, rising toward the bridges like mist. Is it really so heavy, love's wish for a little eternity? The love locks are gold, evening and morning: there's nothing lighter than light.

Passing Smiles

THEY AREN'T MEANT for us. Sometimes it happens along the sidewalk. There's the smile of *hello*. The greeters pass without stopping and one of them makes his way toward you. For a few seconds, his face retains a glow, bearing no apparent relation to the absolute brevity of his encounter. They didn't even take time to exchange a *how are you?* Nothing seems to justify this mask of floating happiness, as if life were suddenly very beautiful. Then you get to watch that zygomatic exaggeration vanish. It's always a surprise. In a fraction of a second, not the slightest trace of what seemed inextinguishable delight, directed toward both the fruit stand and your own approaching figure.

On the metro or the train, there's the text smile. Of course, you're spying on the person focused on her mobile phone, but this intrusion is allowed by the rules of the game if your gaze doesn't linger, pretends to keep scanning a respectable range. To smile at receiving a text message seems normal, almost commonplace. But to smile when writing one gives the space a different texture. You catch in this trespass a virtual complicity, expectant and deferred, that belies the feverish tapping and begins to hover in the car's hostile, sweltering heat. Joke or endearment? You don't know, but you envy the exultation of the sender.

There's also the smile of those who are reading or listening to music. A furtive little gleam that accompanies a sentence, words of a song.

All these smiles appearing randomly, anonymously, in the din, in a crowd. It's so patently human and yet so subtle, a show of abandon that creates further secrecy, distance. And that leaves us a little more bereft, having just brushed up against it.

Awesome!

A T THE END of gladiatorial combat, Roman emperors raised
a thumb to spare the life of the defeated gladiator or
lowered it to condemn him. Much later, in schoolyards, the
raised thumb during a game of tag signaled a truce. These days,
a thumbs up has become hyperbolic, expressing admiration
beyond words. Nevertheless there can be a paradoxical nuance
to this superlative form of enthusiasm. It involves a moment
in soccer games that recurs frequently.

A striker breaks free, in hopes of getting a pass or a center delivered by a teammate. But the ball is intercepted by a
defender, or flies well past the striker, out of reach. The usual
impetuousness of soccer players would logically inspire a gesture of annoyance, or at least a show of disappointment after

that useless run. But strangely, the frustrated player then turns toward the bungling teammate and offers an incongruous thumbs up.

This isn't a matter of ironic congratulations, which the passer might just deserve. No, it's much friendlier, apparently—and actually a bit more calculating, perhaps. With this falsely triumphant raised thumb, our striker celebrates the excellence of intention alone. Yes, it's great that you tried to direct that pass to me. And above all, despite this first failure, keep your eye on me, keep calling on me, I depend on your good will, don't be discouraged. Here we approach the finest subtleties of the game, which is, of course, collective, yet in which all players have their individual roles, protect their own interests, and play their personal career cards.

If I want to score goals, you must send me passes. With a thumbs up, I'm using the language of admiration to express entreaty. This also means, send passes to me rather than to someone else; we're signing a kind of acknowledgment of debt here, too.

The stakes of professional soccer can prompt unnatural,

inauthentic reactions, as well as crazes such as this, with children and amateurs on soccer fields everywhere restaging the drama, raising a thumb to salute the intention of a pass, however approximate. Awesome: you blew it!

Gazing at Your Whisky

IN BLACK-AND-WHITE Hollywood westerns and detective films, characters down their whiskys in a single gulp without even glancing at the glass. It's funny. You can't say that all those shots of bourbon tossed back in a disillusioned, masculine gesture don't fuel your desire to conform to the ritual. And nevertheless you do the exact opposite.

You're immobile, comfortably settled in an armchair at evening's end. The overactivity of cowboys and gangsters has been drowned in the golden amber. All that remains is a delinquent suggestion of virility. No ice, no water. A wide glass and a seemingly reasonable ration—you immediately stop the hand that's pouring. Whisky is an idea, an alchemy. You contemplate it with satisfaction. The Al Capones and John Waynes have disappeared. What supersedes them: Scotland and Ireland. Unemployment, smoke from factories, red smokestacks, heavy clouds scudding over open country alternately opaque and phosphorescent green, almost black under the rain, dazzling and velvety with the least ray of sun. The word *peat* offers its weight of vegetal confusion to the gaze you rest on those two fingers of deceptive horizontality. Other rugged words combine with it to add a bitter, jagged edge, the spell of muted, concave notes: Talisker, Aberlour.

To gaze at your whisky is to be amazed that the tonality of sunlit autumn can harbor so many menacing shadows, that such perfect serenity can engulf so many unleashed winds. You really feel it. With the first swallows this savagery will surge and break, even while you retain a mask of impassivity. You're in no hurry. You founder, you contemplate. You drown.

The Leather of Hazel Wood

I T'S BOTH MORE and less than a present. In the era of video games, it could seem a little anachronistic to give a child a carved stick. But if he's at the age of "let's pretend," the age of duels and stories about knights, there's still hope. This is a gift to a childhood as much as to a child—a gift you're making to yourself.

You know you have to find a branch of hazel wood. There's deep satisfaction in thinking to yourself that the Opinel No. 6 you always carry in your pocket will be of use. You sit down on a big rock. The first incision is not too bold. Just a thin ring to mark the hilt of the sword. Hazel bark is like delicate leather. It has tiny wrinkles, a few pale spots, a suppleness that you haven't forgotten. You must keep the hand light and trace two parallel rings deep enough to prevent you from going beyond them afterwards, when you begin to cut into the bark. Hidden under the brown is a pale green, a ligneous protection that covers the white, almost wet wood. It's very sweet to reach it, having done no harm.

Now you grasp the blade firmly and begin to work meticulously. As you carve, you're watching yourself carve—it's both so rare and such a rite, this vegetal movement. It's as if you had within you every field, every stream, April in all its brilliance under the clear sky, all the daisies, all the dandelions in blossom. The first circle is a success. You make two, then three of them, you try a row of block letters, hieroglyphs, a bit like on a totem pole. Then you're ready to go, to sinusoidalize, to embellish. Millimeter by millimeter, letter by letter, you trace an entire first name. You really botch a few curves, you leave a little green, you cut to the wood in the belly of the *c*, which you widen to hide the mistake—too bad, the *c* will be too fat. The afternoon advances, you feel proud of all the time you've passed. Passed but not lost, no, won, and won again.

The Pavane of Folded Sheets

—Y OU WANT TO help me fold the sheets?

Folding the sheets. There's something special in those three words. A serenity. After the sheets are folded, they're stacked in the closet. Their freshness is tucked away in the dark, their clean scent a forgotten secret. But first, there's this dance to do: one of you steps back, opposite the other, as for a pavane. It doesn't matter if you've never danced it. You feel the ancestral choreography of this folding, this silent dialogue, in your whole body. To find the right distance is a step-by-step challenge. You don't say "stand back a little," you suggest it with a nod of the head. Both arms raised, you feel like both the village yokel and court nobility.

The style is courtly but energetic. The movement for drawing the fabric taut makes it snap like a flag. There's always a hint of reproach in the first adjustment, a little jerk of the wrist that will tolerate no laxness. Then comes a rhythm, followed by a harmony, with the folding into fourths, into eighths. Finally, the cloth is square and smooth, and you can look up at each other. You're going to move closer, but not at the same time. One of you must take the first step. But there's no hesitation. After that first slightly gruff nod, an accord was reached, an ease set in, a shared fluidity. You know which of you must wait, which of you must advance. That's part of the dance, and more.

Banner Kite

THE VERY HEART of summer. Stretched out on the beach, you've done your duty. An energetic contribution to the construction of a sandcastle, the walls inlaid with shells, and even a flag made from a twig poked through a small leaf. On your back, with a clear conscience, you close your eyes. The cries of children grow distant and fade as the surf begins its syncopated lullaby.

Did you fall asleep for a bit? It's hard to tell, time has become insubstantial. In any case, you can't say if the rumbling that woke you comes from overhead. It really seems to originate within, from a desire to experience the sensation of space by mastering the sky. No, it's not an ultralight. You sit up, lean back on your elbows. Half opening your eyes, you're surprised to find the entire beach so quietly stunned. Sand shovels suspended mid-air, readers looking up from their crime novels, busy knitting needles stilled. Despite its persistent mosquito-like rage, this flimsy biplane is not announcing a bombardment. Instead it unfurls a long ribbon of white cloth, and this message, shuddering between gusts of wind, becomes legible: "Intermarché. Now open every Sunday from 9 to 1."

Such important news, you have to admit, to bring young and old out of their torpor, break their concentration. You'd love to tell the sky it doesn't matter. But the message flapping up there really is the one you've been waiting for. You knew that the Intermarché was open on Sundays, but you wanted to know it like this, carried on the momentum of a tiny club plane resurging from another era. Its passing expands the cosmic void of the word *vacation*. There's surprising comfort in being disturbed in this way, by a falsely momentous rumble. The advertising technique employed is so spectacularly outworn that it says exactly the opposite of what it says. Which everyone pretends to read and is forgetting already, gazing off into the slightly milky sky as the banner becomes a kite.

The Ecstasy of the Selfie

O F COURSE there are those telescopic selfie sticks for hold-ing your phone at almost any angle, for photos of couples or groups posing at some tourist site. It's a familiar expedient of innocent and accepted tourism, in front of Mont Saint-Michel or in gondolas. But in the cultural tsunami of the selfie, the basic gesture remains the extended arm—stretched as far away from you as possible.

You can do it as a friendly gesture: I've taken photos of myself with Zidane, Macron, Bruel. The celebrities in this world are always flattered; they count on such shots. More essential and more specious, is the arm extended in solitude to photograph oneself. There's still a vague alibi to rely on here—if I send this out over the Internet, you'll be able to see in the background

Piccadilly Circus or the Louvre Pyramid, the reason for my trip, for your mild surprise. But more and more frequently the hand is outstretched to capture only the self. A flattering self-image at the end of a tensed arm. An exaltation of one's own face—with a little training, the dazzling smile, the enigmatic or sensual pose can require just a fraction of a second. Before and after comes something like surprise, maybe anxiety. So quickly dispelled, so quick to return. Why such a need to find ourselves attractive? Which in some cases seems obvious, in others nearly impossible. Still, less attractive faces don't deny themselves this angelic rapture.

Psychologists are having a field day. Here's their whole lineup, the id, the ego, the self, all staging this drama of images. But what part do I play? Do I invent myself a little to gain distance from myself, to extend my arm? Do I draw near to draw back? Do I exist?

Crossing Your Hands Behind Your Back

IT'S ESPECIALLY MEN who do this. Old, or rather older, leaner ones—stout ones are reluctant to put their bellies on display. Maybe they adopt this posture because they grew up in a time when keeping one's hands in one's pockets was a sign of poor upbringing. But above all, clasping your hands behind your back is like proof of freedom and detachment. They take small steps, they stop. They want to be struck somehow by a sight that will warrant standing still—but it's much less a matter of curiosity than fatigue.

Hands crossed behind their backs, they've become spectators. Their days of exertion are over, although the marks of it are visible in their stooped silhouettes, their slightly stiff gait. Flea markets are good for them because stops are justified for subjects that are most often pure pretext. It's not too awkward to ask that little girl if she's really selling her dolls. It's much easier, of course, to comment on the use of a farm tool or mechanical device, exchanging familiar, noncommittal remarks on progress.

Hands crossed behind their backs, they nod their heads or smile, and then go on their way. They aren't moralists and they aren't bitter. They're grateful to the world for existing without them, and for letting them draw close, as if they were part of the game. They're courteous in their way of asking for nothing, of reproaching nothing, of wearing carefully ironed shirts with sleeves they won't roll up even in mid-summer. The years have passed much too quickly up till now, but it's lucky to have had years, they aren't complaining.

Hands crossed behind their backs, they wouldn't say there was nothing interesting at the flea market. They just left.

È finita la scuola!

J UNE 9, that might seem very early. But it's true that here in Venice, they've already transitioned to summer. Since morning, in one square or another, you can hear rising from behind walls waves of songs, applause, laughter. The last day of school for the primary grades! At noon, the children pour out in perfect safety. The squares and narrow streets belong to them, just as they belong to the old people. No risk of cars, motorcycles, bikes. The body fears nothing. You hear all their voices, and especially these: higher, louder. The fluty voices of five children, three girls and two boys, drunk on freedom. They must be six or seven years old. In the winding street that leads to Campo San Margarita, they suddenly fan out in a movement of spontaneous exhilaration. They take each other by the hand

and run, pleased with their audacity that prompts only smiles, amused fondness, a little envy. Which of them starts singing it first? *"È finita la scuola!"*

A few basic notes, but their exuberance creates a harmony. A collective victory that seems without rancor toward school— you'd love to be the teacher of children like these. It's more a bright hymn to the idea of summer vacation. It's less the end of something than elation over the present, which finds in them its cadence, its music, its song, and especially this lovely movement, hand in hand, weaving across the whole width of the alley. Life is good on June 9 at high noon in the streets of Venice. You watch them. You feel better. And why suddenly think of Ionesco's king who repeats: "I want to go back to school!"?

Rolling Up Your Sleeves

FOR SOME TIME, it remains a possibility that you resist. There's a certain pleasure in keeping long sleeves buttoned, especially since fashion encourages leaving shirttails untucked to hang over one's pants. It's cotton or linen, of course. No banker's stripes escaping the confines of a suit. The "slim fit" line proclaimed by the label invites you to make the shirt a little fashion statement all on its own.

So the sleeves stay buttoned as long as possible. You remain a cool, respectable figure, undaunted by the heat. You have class, but you're not ostentatious—others can tell you detest polo shirts worn with the collar turned up.

Even while you're talking, walking along, you can feel your-self gradually giving in to the temptation. It's the gesture that prompts the desire: to undo the button and turn back the cuff just above the wrist, nowhere close to the elbow. It's more a mental proposition than a physical exercise. Just the semblance of a French cuff can save you from perfect rectitude and restraint. In the heat of a discussion, this can signal half-consciously that you're entitled to your own opinion. If you're walking alone, it's with the surroundings that you get a little more casual. Two turns over the forearm, no more, but you're a different creature in the world, a free man, something of an artist, who manages the feat of maintaining a balance between laid-back and sophisticated.

A delicate balance. That first roll of the sleeve is always a bit loose, and the fabric wants to come unrolled again. You redo it two or three times because you've got a weakness for this little half-measure of seduction.

And then it gets too hot, you're too encumbered. So you roll, or you refold. Above the elbow. That stays put, but it's something else altogether. Can you retain your elegance? Or rather, at best, a slightly retro image from films on the Liberation, the Spanish Civil War—a leftist style, that's some consolation. Already you're tempted to unroll, to rebutton.

In a shirt, you can be many things. It's good having more than one trick up your sleeve.

The Morning Leans Down

YOU'RE WALKING HIM to school in the morning. It's odd; in late afternoon, there isn't this same inclination, the same desire for shared secrecy. On the other hand, there's more to ask about, elicit, listen to. But the morning walk to school makes you lean down. You're not too early, the school is just ahead, and you're going to leave him there. A few minutes on the sidewalk, the city's cool rumble just beginning to build. Do you regret no longer being a child? No, not really, you're pretty content with what you have to do, a whole day ahead of you, appointments, lots of plans. In the morning Sisyphus is lucky to have a stone to roll. But you have infinite respect for the idea of his school day. It's so much more serious, all the novelty of that world he's going to have to tame, letter by letter, page by page.

You don't talk to him about school and he won't mention it either. What matters is being together, exchanging easy words, holding his hand, or not, leaning over him. It's strange: you gather him in because you're moving forward. The intense protectiveness of this posture would be indecent if you were holding still. But there's tacit agreement: he likes it, he lets you bend toward him as he walks tall, his pack on his back. You know it would spoil everything if you were to carry his things. You are two parallel, complicit destinies. The traffic noise from cars, but especially motorbikes and scooters, compels this position if you want to understand each other. You understand each other.

Cruel and Tender Life

YOU EMBRACE, just like that, on the sidewalk of an empty street or along a remote seaside trail—you didn't hear the dog coming, its owner following behind, you pretend not to see them. You remain intent on each other. Over forty years you've lived together, and still there's this desire to embrace as soon as some out-of-the-way place restores a complicit freedom. You remember reading in a little book of sayings, "Two in silence, that's happiness." You look up to gaze into each other's eyes for a few seconds. A long interrogation, approaching anxiety, and just at the end a glimmer of a smile, as though to mock yourself, yourselves, a little—maybe it's both very serious and very child-ish to hug like this when you share every ounce of daily life.

But no, two in silence is not happiness. You feel that when

you release your gaze and gently caress, the sensation of the other's body. No, it's very good, but it's not really tranquil. You couldn't be closer, more loving, more one. And nevertheless, it's the fragility that you feel. Between us, the past. Is it really certain, all that we've experienced? When we need or long to embrace like this, all those fleeting days are not amassed treasure, we have no key to the treasure chest, there is no treasure chest. The long way we've come seems so tenuous, and somehow threatened by the ascending present. It's still our adolescence, our least word might be laughable.

How many evenings are left for us to surprise each other so, to slowly start walking again, taking each other's hand? Soon to feel the need to say something stupid. To pretend not to be taken in and to worry at the deepest level about this fickle bit of luck—the surest moment is also the most amazed, the least possessable. We'll never know. Life is tender. And cruel.

archipelago books
is a not-for-profit literary press devoted to
promoting cross-cultural exchange through innovative
classic and contemporary international literature
www.archipelagobooks.org